This book belongs to

- -

Bluebell Glade

Dandelion Dell

Heart of Misty Wood

Hawthorn Hedgerows

Heather Hill

Sundown Hill

Crystal Cave

Golden Meadow

Moonshine Pond

Dewdrop Spring

Honeydew Meadow

Mulberry Bushes

Misty Wood Rabbit Warren

HOME SWEET HOME

How many Fairy Animals books have you collected?

- ❀ Chloe the Kitten
- ✓ Bella the Bunny
- ❀ Paddy the Puppy
- ❀ Mia the Mouse

And there are more magical adventures coming very soon!

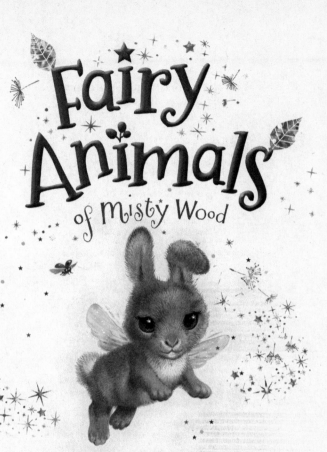

Fairy Animals
of Misty Wood

Bella the Bunny

Lily Small

Henry Holt and Company
New York

With special thanks to Thea Bennett

Henry Holt and Company, LLC
Publishers since 1866
175 Fifth Avenue
New York, New York 10010
mackids.com

Henry Holt® is a registered trademark of
Henry Holt and Company, LLC.
Text copyright © 2013 by Hothouse Fiction Ltd.
Illustrations copyright © 2013 by Artful Doodlers Ltd.
Cover illustration © John Francis
All rights reserved.

First published in the United States in 2015
by Henry Holt and Company, LLC.
Originally published in Great Britain in 2013
by Egmont UK Limited.

Library of Congress Cataloging-in-Publication Data
Small, Lily.
Bella the bunny / Lily Small. — First American edition.
pages cm. — (Fairy animals of Misty Wood ; [2])
Summary: Bella, a fairy rabbit, helps Lexi the ladybug understand that if she does her
best she will be judged on what she accomplishes, rather than on her appearance.
ISBN 978-1-62779-142-7 (paperback) — ISBN 978-1-62779-361-2 (e-book)
[1. Fairies—Fiction. 2. Rabbits—Fiction. 3. Ladybugs—Fiction.
4. Self-confidence—Fiction.] I. Title.
PZ7.S635Bel 2015   [Fic]—dc23   2014039993

Henry Holt books may be purchased for business or promotional use. For information on
bulk purchases, please contact the Macmillan Corporate and Premium Sales Department
at (800) 221-7945 x5442 or by e-mail at specialmarkets@macmillan.com.

First American Edition—2015
Printed in the United States of America by R. R. Donnelley &
Sons Company, Harrisonburg, Virginia

5 7 9 10 8 6 4

Contents

Chapter One
The Talking Bud   1

Chapter Two
A Sad Ladybug   20

Chapter Three
Wanted: Spots!   35

Chapter Four
Daydreaming   51

Chapter Five
Magic Toadstools   63

Chapter Six
Moonshine Pond to Heather Hill   80

Chapter Seven
Loop-the-Loop   103

CHAPTER ONE

The Talking Bud

Spring had come to Misty Wood.
The early morning sun could see
lots of baby plants starting to grow
on the ground below as he rose

through the bright blue sky. With a warm smile, the sun reached out his beams to help the plants push through the soil.

High among the trees, there was a flash of silver. It was a little bunny! She had soft silver-gray fur, violet eyes that sparkled like jewels . . . and a pair of golden fairy wings. Her name was Bella, and she was a Bud Bunny—one of the fairy animals who lived in Misty Wood.

As she flitted through the trees, she sang a song about the special job she was going to do—open the beautiful spring flowers.

Shine on, shine on, big, bright sun!

I'm on my way to have some fun.

I'll be spending happy hours

Turning buds into flowers!

Suddenly, Bella felt something trickle down her fur. Droplets of rain had started to fall. *Pitter-patter* went the raindrops as they bounced on

4

the leaves. Bella smiled as the water tickled her nose. She liked the rain just as much as she liked the sun—it helped the flowers to grow, too!

Bella twitched her velvety nose. The leaves and the earth and the new plants smelled lovely in the rain. Everything was green and fresh.

Misty Wood will be even more beautiful when I've done my job! Bella thought. She twirled her wings and did a happy somersault. *Soon*

there'll be lovely flowers everywhere!

Just as quickly as it had begun, the rain stopped and the sun was shining again.

"No time to lose," Bella told herself. "I must hurry to Bluebell Glade. There are hundreds of bluebells there, just waiting for me to open them."

She darted off through the trees, singing more of her song.

Little buds just wait for me.

I'll come soon to help you be

Pretty flowers fresh and bright,

Blue and yellow, pink and white.

"Hello, Bella!"

Bella spun around at the sound

of her name. Carla, a Cobweb

Kitten, was flying along behind

her. Her wings sparkled in the

sunlight as she hurried to catch up.

Carla was Bella's best friend.

She had white fur the same color

as the mist that gathered under

7

the trees—and beautiful spots that
looked like chocolate chips.

Carla flew up, and the two
friends touched noses to say hello.

"I can't stop. I must get to
Bluebell Glade," Bella explained.
Then she noticed the little basket

Carla was carrying, made from tightly woven flower stems. "Your basket looks heavy today, Carla."

"It's full to the brim with dewdrops," Carla replied proudly.

Just like the Bud Bunnies, the Cobweb Kittens had an important job to do in Misty Wood. Every day, the Cobweb Kittens gathered dewdrops and hung them on cobwebs so they glittered in the sunlight.

Suddenly, Bella's ears quivered.
She could hear a buzzing noise.

Bzzzzzzzz. Bzzzzzzzzzzz.

"What's that?" Bella said,
spinning around.

"Look!" Carla cried.

Bella turned to see what Carla
had spotted. A cloud of tiny wings
glinted in the sunshine. Hundreds
of insects were flying toward them.

A small blue June bug bumped
into Bella's nose.

"Oops, sorry!" the June bug squeaked before whizzing on.

Then a swarm of striped hoverflies buzzed by.

"Hey, where are you going?" called Carla.

"*Zzzzz.* Musssst dassshhhh!" the hoverflies replied, following the June bug.

"I've never seen so many insects," Bella told Carla. "I wonder what's going on."

A big yellow butterfly fluttered up to them.

"Hello, Mr. Butterfly," Bella said. "Where are you all going?"

"Today is the Misty Wood Insect Sports Day," he said. "I'm the chief steward!" He twirled his long antennae grandly.

"Wow!" Bella gasped.

"Insect Sports Day! How could we have forgotten?" said Carla. "It happens every year on Heather Hill."

"Do come along. Everyone's welcome," the friendly butterfly

13

said before whooshing after the hoverflies.

"Oh, I wish we could go," Carla sighed. "Watching the insects race must be so much fun!"

"I know!" said Bella. "Maybe we can, if we're really quick with our cobwebs and flower buds."

"Great idea!" Carla exclaimed. "I'd better start hanging up these dewdrops, then. Bye, Bella. See you later at Heather Hill." Carla

rubbed noses with her friend and flew off toward the edge of the wood, where the cobwebs were waiting for their dewdrops.

"Bye!" Bella called after her. Then she set off toward Bluebell Glade, humming her happy song.

When Bella reached the glade, she swooped down and landed among the bluebells. Each one had lots of tight green buds just waiting to be opened. Bella's nose tingled

with excitement. When she finished her work, the glade would be a sea of blue, and the sweet smell of the flowers would drift all through Misty Wood.

She hopped over to a bluebell stem and twitched her nose against the biggest bud. Very slowly, the petals began to unfurl. Bella hopped back and watched, her whiskers quivering in delight. This was her favorite part of her job. It was

like watching a beautiful present
unwrap itself. She held her breath,
and a pretty blue flower, the same
shape as a fairy's cap, burst out.

Bella sang happily as she
hopped and bounced her way over
to another bud.

A hippity-hop and a hoppity-hip.

Opening flowers makes me skip!

Soon she had opened dozens
of bluebells. They tinkled like
bells in the breeze, and the glade

17

was filled with their sweet scent.

Then there was just one flower left to open. Bella hopped over to it eagerly. One more flower and then she could go to Insect Sports Day! But just as she placed her velvety nose next to the bud, something very strange happened.

"Please don't!" a voice squeaked.

Bella hopped back on her heels and stared at the plant in shock. The voice was coming from the

flower! In all the time she'd been a
Bud Bunny, Bella had never heard
a bud speak to her before. What
was going on?

CHAPTER TWO

A Sad Ladybug

Bella pricked up her ears and listened. Everything was quiet. Maybe she'd imagined the voice.

"After all, buds can't talk,

or can they?" she said to herself.

She hopped up close to the bluebell again. She was about to touch her nose to the bud when—

"Didn't you hear what I said?" the bud squeaked. "Please, please leave me alone!"

Bella jumped back in surprise. She definitely hadn't imagined the voice this time.

"Don't open me," the flower pleaded. Its voice was quivery

now—as if it was about to cry.

"Why ever not?" Bella asked.

The bud went quiet again.

Bella leaned in close. "Don't you want to be a pretty flower?" she whispered.

The bud made a noise that sounded like a sigh. Then it said, in a teeny-tiny voice, "Well . . . the thing is . . ."

"I can't hear you," Bella said.

The voice spoke again, a bit

22

louder now. "The thing is . . . you see . . . I like being a bud. I don't want to change."

Bella's ears shot up and her eyes opened wide. She couldn't believe what the flower was saying. "Don't be silly!" she said. "You'll be a beautiful bluebell!"

"No!" squeaked the bud.

But Bella's nose was already twitching. The bud was probably just shy. Once Bella had opened

23

it, and the flower saw how lovely
it looked, it would soon change its
mind. She pressed her nose against
the bud and wiggled it.

One by one, the shiny blue
petals unpeeled to reveal the
biggest, brightest bluebell in the
whole glade.

"There, see. You're beautiful!"
Bella cried, clapping her silky paws.

"No!" the voice wailed. "I'm not
beautiful at all. Look at me!"

Something flew out of the flower, zoomed toward Bella, and landed on her nose. Bella squinted to see what was there.

It was a tiny ladybug! She had a tiny frown on her face.

"Why didn't you listen to me?" the ladybug whispered. "Why couldn't you leave me in there?"

"I'm really sorry." Bella's ears flopped down over her face, the way they always did when she felt upset. "I . . . I thought it was the flower talking."

"But flowers don't talk!" the ladybug exclaimed.

"I know, but . . ." Now Bella frowned. "What were you doing

26

hiding inside a bluebell bud?" she asked.

The ladybug looked sad. "I was hiding from Insect Sports Day."

"What? But why?" Bella asked. "Sports Day is fun. I'm going to see it with my friend Carla."

The ladybug flew down from Bella's nose and landed on top of the bluebell in front of her.

"How can I go when I look like this?"

Bella stared at the ladybug. "What's wrong?" she asked. "You look all right to me."

The ladybug sighed. "How many spots can you see?"

Bella peered closely. The little insect was as red and shiny as a juicy apple. Right in the middle of her back was a single black spot.

"Oh!" Bella said. "You have only *one* spot."

The ladybug's eyes filled with

tears. "Exactly! How can I go to Sports Day with just one spot? I'll look stupid!"

"It's a *nice* spot," Bella said.

The ladybug shook her head. "Proper ladybugs have lots of spots. I'm the only ladybug I know with just one. My family knows I'm different. They love me all the same. I don't even mind when my friends call me One-Spot. But"— the ladybug stopped to catch her

29

breath—"if I go to Sports Day, *all* the insects in Misty Wood will see me, and they'll laugh." The ladybug's lip trembled. Her eyes were bright with tears.

"Don't be sad," Bella said.

"How can I not be sad?" the ladybug replied.

Bella's violet eyes lit up. "I know! I'll help you find some more spots."

The ladybug looked confused. "How will you do that?"

"Hmm. Let me think." Bella crouched down and leaned her head to one side to help her brain work better. She wiggled her nose— sometimes that helped her think.

Suddenly, her whiskers twitched, and she hopped in the air.

"We need a song! I never do anything without a song."

Bella hopped and skipped around the little insect. Then she started to sing, thumping her paws on the ground to keep the rhythm.

This ladybug needs some spots.
Hoppity, hoppity, hop!
We're going to find lots and lots.

Hoppity, hoppity, hop!

Hopping here and hopping there,

Hopping, bopping everywhere!

She'll be happy when she's got

LOTS AND LOTS OF SPOTS!

"How was that?" Bella asked, giving an extra-bouncy hop as she finished singing. But there was no reply.

The ladybug had vanished!

34

CHAPTER THREE

Wanted: Spots!

"Don't worry, I'm up here!" a little

voice cried from high in the air.

Bella peered into the sky.

The ladybug zoomed down past

her nose. "Wheeee!" she squealed, whizzing up again and making a big circle in the air.

"Wow! Loop-the-loops!" Bella cried, sitting up on her hind legs to watch as the tiny insect whizzed around again.

"I always do loops when I'm happy," said the ladybug, swooping down to rest on a bluebell stem. "I'm so excited you're going to help me. Thank you!"

"You're welcome. I'm excited, too! By the way, my name is Bella."

"I'm Lexi!" said the ladybug.

"It's lovely to meet you, Lexi. Right. Let's get started," Bella said.

"Hurray!" said Lexi, swinging from the bluebell stem, her eyes shining.

"Now, let me think." Bella tilted her head and wiggled her nose. "Spots . . . spots," she muttered to herself. "Where can we find some spots?"

Then she jumped up, her long whiskers quivering. "I know! My

best friend, Carla, has lots of beautiful spots. Let's go and ask her where they came from."

Lexi didn't say anything. She looked down at the ground.

"What's wrong?" Bella asked.

"I'm scared." Lexi's voice shook as she spoke. "We might bump into some of the insects who are going to Sports Day. They'll laugh at my one stupid spot, and . . . oh . . . it'll be awful!"

"Don't be afraid!" Bella said kindly. "We'll think of something." She leaned her head to one side again to think. How could they find Carla without anyone seeing Lexi? One of Bella's long ears flopped down and touched the ground.

Bella grinned. She had the answer! "Look, Lexi." Bella lifted her silky ear with her paw. "You can hide under here."

"Ooh, yes!" Lexi flew over and

40

crawled under Bella's ear. There was lots of room, and as Lexi nestled into Bella's soft fur, she felt cozy and safe.

Bella gently flapped her golden fairy wings and floated up into the sunlight. She headed for the edge of Misty Wood, where the cobwebs hung thickly on the tall hedgerows. That was where Carla would be.

Carla looked very surprised when

she saw Bella. "I thought you were going to Bluebell Glade," she said.

"I was—and I did—but I need to ask you something," Bella replied, fluttering down to land beside her friend. "Something really important."

Carla blinked her big green eyes. She looked puzzled. "All right. Just let me finish this."

Bella watched as Carla hung some of her dewdrops on a cobweb

that stretched along the top of
the hedge. The dewdrops shone
and sparkled, and the spider silk
glittered like a diamond necklace.

"What's happening?" Lexi
whispered. "I can't see." She started
wriggling about under Bella's ear.

"Shh!" Bella whispered. "And
keep still. You're tickling me!"

Carla glanced around. "I'm
not tickling you," she said, looking
confused. "How can I be tickling

43

you when I'm over here hanging up my dewdrops?"

Bella frowned. "No, not you. I . . . I meant my nose was tickling me. I think I need to sneeze." She rubbed her nose with her front paws.

"Are you okay?" Carla's big eyes widened with concern.

"I'm fine. Look." Bella hopped and skipped a couple of steps, just to prove it.

Carla placed her basket on the

44

mossy ground. "So, what did you want to ask me?"

"Well, we . . . I mean . . . *I* was wondering, where did you get your spots?" Bella asked.

"My spots?" Carla looked down

at the chocolate-colored markings on her snowy white fur.

"Yes. They're so lovely. Where did they come from?" Bella said.

"I've always had them, ever since I was a tiny kitten," Carla replied. "I've no idea where they came from."

Bella heard Lexi sigh under her ear.

"Don't worry," Bella whispered to Lexi. "We'll find someone in

Misty Wood who can help."

"Help with what?" Carla stared at Bella.

"Oh, nothing! Thank you for trying, Carla. See you soon!" Bella hopped away along the hedgerow.

"Bye!" called Carla, still looking confused. "See you later, at Insect Sports Day!"

Bella patted her ear to check that Lexi was safely tucked away. Then, with a rustle and a shimmer

of her golden wings, she took off
and soared toward the middle of
Misty Wood.

Honeydew Meadow spread out
below them. Bella could see some
golden Pollen Puppies darting
about like sunbeams as they did
their special job: spreading the
pollen to make the flowers grow.
But not one of the puppies had any
spots.

Next, Bella flew toward

Dandelion Dell. In the clearing

next to the dell, she caught sight

of something moving. It was a

graceful Dream Deer with long legs and huge eyes. His smooth brown coat and gauzy wings were dappled all over with silvery spots.

"I think I've found someone!" Bella cried. "Hang on tight, Lexi!"

Bella fluttered down to where the deer was nibbling on the sweet spring grass. Surely if anyone could help Lexi, it would be a Dream Deer.

50

CHAPTER FOUR

Daydreaming

The Dream Deer lifted his nose
from the grass and gazed at Bella
with kind brown eyes.

"Are you searching for a dream,

little bunny?" he asked Bella.

Like all the fairy animals in
Misty Wood, the Dream Deer had
their own special job. When the
other animals were sleeping, the
deer brought them happy dreams.

Bella yawned. The deer's voice
was so soft and gentle it made her
feel like taking a nap. She flopped
down on the grass.

"Oh, dear," she said. "I think
I'm falling asleep."

52

"No!" Lexi cried in her ear.

"Please do," the deer said in his velvety voice. "I have a lovely dream for you."

"Noooo!" Lexi cried again.

But as Bella's eyes closed, the ladybug's voice began to fade. The Dream Deer's magic was working.

Bella dreamed she was opening buds high in the treetops. But she'd never seen flowers like these before.

They were huge white blossoms, hanging like brightly shining moons.

"Please don't go to sleep!" a little voice squeaked in Bella's ear. "What about my spots?"

But Bella was lost in her dream, and she didn't hear Lexi at all.

Now she could see that the white flowers were dotted with gold and yellow and silver. They had lots and lots of beautiful spots.

"Spots!" Bella called out, opening her eyes and jumping up.

"Hurray!" Lexi cried.

The deer looked at Bella, surprised. "Didn't you like your dream?" he asked.

"I loved it," Bella told him. "But I can't sleep now. I need to find some spots. Where did *your* spots come from?"

The deer flicked his tail and turned his long neck to look at the

silvery spots on his fur and wings.

"I don't know," he said.

"They've always been there."

Bella heard Lexi give another

sad little sigh in her ear. Bella

tried not to show the deer how

disappointed she was. "Oh well. Thank you anyway. And thanks for the lovely dream."

The deer smiled warmly. "I'm very sorry I wasn't able to help you," he said. "I do hope you find some spots, whatever they are for." Then he leaped gracefully into the air and soared away.

"What are we going to do now?" Lexi whispered.

"I don't know," Bella said. She

was beginning to feel a *tiny* bit worried, too.

"You could try another song," Lexi suggested.

"Good idea." Bella jumped up and began hopping along a little path that led through the trees. Lexi snuggled back under Bella's ear. After a moment, Bella began to sing.

Hop-a-long, hop-a-long,
hoppity-hop!

We're looking for someone to give

us some spots.

A Dream Deer couldn't help us,

And neither could a kitten!

So we're searching the wood

For where they are hidden!

Bella kept hopping and singing.

The path led deep into the Heart of Misty Wood. The trees grew close together, and the ferns and moss were thick and green.

Bella felt a little afraid. Apart from her song, this part of the wood was silent. There was no one around, and no sign of *any* spots!

Oh, dear. I must be going the wrong way, Bella thought.

She was about to turn and hop back when a ray of sunshine lit the

path ahead. The trees thinned as
she hopped into a clearing.

Bella came to a halt, her heart
beating fast. There was a ring of
bright red toadstools in the clearing.

"Why have you stopped?" Lexi
asked.

Bella raised her ear so that

Lexi could see the toadstools.

"Mushrooms?" Lexi said. "How can mushrooms help us?"

"They're not mushrooms. They're *toadstools*!" Bella explained.

Lexi was very puzzled.

"It's a magic toadstool ring!" Bella whispered. "A place where wishes come true!"

And without another word, she hopped out of the trees and flew straight to the middle of the ring.

CHAPTER FIVE

Magic Toadstools

It was very quiet in the middle of the toadstool ring. There were no birds singing, and even the leaves in the trees had stopped rustling. Bella

gave a little shiver, but she knew she must be brave. She raised her ear right up.

"Come and sit beside me," she whispered to Lexi.

"Why?" Lexi asked.

"We need to close our eyes," Bella explained. "Then I'll make a wish for you to have some spots."

"Oh, I hope it works," breathed Lexi.

Bella closed her eyes tight and

thought for a moment. As soon as the words came into her head, she began to sing.

> *Lexi's only got one spot,*
> *Which makes her feel so sad.*
> *But grant my wish, kind toadstools,*
> *And she'll be very glad!*

Bella stopped singing and listened. There was still no sound. Not even the faintest breeze or quietest birdsong. But then . . . *swoosh!*

Something ruffled against her.

"What's that?" Lexi squeaked.

Swish! Swoosh!

There it was again. It felt as if a big, soft brush was stroking Bella's fur.

"Don't move!" Bella whispered to Lexi. "It's the magic. You have to keep your eyes closed."

Suddenly, the swooshing stopped. Everything was quiet.

Bella opened one eye and saw

the ring of toadstools. Then she
opened her other eye.

"Oh no!" she gasped when she
saw Lexi.

"Oh no!" squeaked Lexi when
she saw Bella.

"What's wrong?" they both said
at exactly the same time.

"You've got spots!" Bella said.
"But—"

"So have you," interrupted Lexi.
"Big white ones!"

Bella stared at the ladybug. "Yours are white, too!"

"They can't be!" Lexi cried.

"It's true," Bella said. "Let's go look in that puddle over there."

They fluttered over to look at their reflections in the water.

"It *is* true!" Lexi said. "I've got lots and lots of white spots. But they should be *black*."

Bella gazed at her friend. The ladybug did look strange, with

one big black spot and lots of little white ones. Then Bella leaned over to look at her own reflection.

"Oh my!" she exclaimed. There were big white blobs all over her silky gray fur. She didn't look like her usual self at all.

Lexi started to cry. Tiny trails of tears glimmered as they trickled down her face. "I c-can't go to Sports Day like this! What are we going to do?"

69

"Don't worry," Bella said. "This
toadstool ring is definitely magic,

but I must have sung the wish wrong. Let me try again."

Bella started flying back toward the ring, but Lexi stayed where she was.

"Why aren't you coming?" Bella asked.

"The magic might go wrong again," Lexi replied. "I might end up with purple spots. Or spots every color of the rainbow. And that would be even worse!"

"I'm sure that won't happen," Bella said, flying back over to Lexi. "I just have to get the wish right. That's all."

Lexi gave a little nod and fluttered back to the toadstool ring.

When they were both in the ring again, they closed their eyes. Bella tilted her head, wiggled her nose, and then started singing.

I should have asked for black spots!
Can the white ones disappear?

72

Lexi needs some black ones.

Oh, I do hope you can hear!

Misty Wood was silent again. Had the song worked? Bella opened one eye to take a peek. Lexi's spots were still white! The toadstools had worked their magic the first time—why weren't they listening now? Bella took a deep breath and bellowed at the top of her voice.

Listen, toadstools, in your ring,

73

Can't you hear me when I sing?

Lexi needs some BLACK SPOTS

And—

"There's no need to shout," a deep voice interrupted.

Bella's fur stood on end, and Lexi squeaked with fright. They both kept their eyes shut tight. Maybe the magic was working?

"I don't do black spots," the voice said. "I do only white."

That doesn't sound very magical,

Bella thought. She opened her eyes.

A large red fox was sitting in front of them. He was holding a lily pad full of white paint.

"Are you *sure* you do only white spots?" Lexi said.

"Quite sure," said the fox, nodding.

"Sorry," said Bella. "But Lexi needs *black* spots."

"Yes," said Lexi. "I'm a ladybug, you see."

The fox stood up and shook himself. "Watch this," he said. Then he trotted over to the edge of the ring with his lily pad. He dipped

his tail in the paint and dabbed one of the red toadstools until it was covered with white spots.

"See?" he said. "That's my job. Putting the white spots on the toadstools."

"Gosh, that looks lovely," Bella said. "Much better than plain red toadstools."

"Thanks," the fox said with a smile. "I'm really sorry I'm not able to help you. And don't worry.

The spots will wash off. I have to repaint these toadstools every time it rains."

He picked up his lily pad and moved on to the next toadstool.

"Good-bye, Mr. Fox. Thank you for trying to help us," Bella said. "Come on, Lexi."

"Where are we going?" Lexi asked as she settled down in Bella's soft fur.

"Moonshine Pond," Bella told

78

her. "We'll wash away these white spots, and then we'll think of what to do next."

"Okay!" squeaked Lexi as the bunny opened her golden wings and fluttered into the air. "Let's go!"

CHAPTER SIX

Moonshine Pond to Heather Hill

"The pond looks so bright and beautiful today," Bella cried as she spotted the gleaming water through

the trees. "The Moonbeam Moles
have been busy."

Every night, the moles caught
moonbeams and dropped them into
Moonshine Pond to make it glow
like the moon itself.

Bella landed on the grassy
bank. "Okay, Lexi, time to wash off
those spots," she called, raising her
ear so Lexi could fly out.

Lexi landed on the bank and
looked down at the silvery water.

"What if they don't wash off?" she said nervously.

"Oh, I'm sure they will. Look." Bella dipped a paw in the edge of the pond. The fox was right—the water washed the white blobs clean away.

"Yippee!" Lexi cried, and she did a quick loop-the-loop before diving headfirst into the water.

Bella hopped in, too, and splashed and splashed until all the spots were gone.

"That's better!" she cried,

leaping onto the bank and shaking

out her fur and wings.

"You look like a proper Bud Bunny again!" said Lexi, crawling out from the water. "Are my spots gone, too?"

"They are," Bella replied. "Only the black one's left."

"I'd better dry myself off," Lexi said. She flew up into the air, whirring her little wings as she loop-the-looped.

Bella sat down on the grass. She felt really sad that she hadn't been

able to help Lexi, but it was lovely
to rest in the sunshine. She could
feel the warm rays drying her fur.

"Wheeee!" came Lexi's voice
from high in the air.

Bella looked up and smiled.
Lexi must be feeling very happy
that the white spots were gone.
She was loop-the-looping again
and again.

Then Bella saw a large yellow
butterfly fluttering through the

trees. It was the same one she and Carla had met that morning.

"Hello again!" the butterfly said, landing on the grass.

"Hello, Mr. Butterfly. I thought you were going to Sports Day," Bella said.

"It's just about to start," the butterfly explained. "As chief steward, it's my job to make sure no insects get left behind. I wouldn't want anyone to miss it!"

Then he saw Lexi loop-the-
looping.

"My, oh my, little ladybug,
what wonderful flying!" he called.
"With talent like that, you should
be racing in Sports Day. Quick,
come with me."

Bella was about to explain
that Lexi was shy, but it was too
late. The butterfly had leaped into
the air.

"Oh, no, no, no!" squealed Lexi,

zooming up to the top of her loop as the butterfly approached.

But the butterfly was in such a hurry that he didn't hear her. He scooped Lexi up in his long legs and swooped off through the trees.

Bella, confused, twitched her nose. Everything had happened so quickly. One moment Lexi was happily loop-the-looping, and the next moment she was gone!

Bella whirled her shining golden

wings and flew after the butterfly as fast as she could.

"Don't worry, Lexi!" she shouted as she took off. "I'm coming!"

"Wow!" Bella gasped as she saw Heather Hill.

Everything was ready for Insect Sports Day. There was a circular flying track for the June bugs and the ladybugs, with lots of obstacles

for them to get over. Flowers had been laid out to make a nectar-gathering marathon for the bees. There was a high jump for the grasshoppers and a cobweb trapeze for the spiders, and some fireflies were marking out an area in the sky for the butterflies' races.

All around the edge of the arena, fairy animals were taking their places, excitedly waiting for Sports Day to begin. The Pollen

Puppies were wagging their tails so fast they blurred. The Stardust Squirrels were scampering about, sprinkling stardust until the heather glittered silver in the sun.

Bella saw a group of Cobweb Kittens sitting under a large oak tree. She wondered if her friend Carla was here already, but she couldn't stop and check now. She had to find out if Lexi was okay.

Bella dived into the crowd of

insects who were hurrying about and pushed her way to the front.

She spotted the yellow butterfly at the start of the flying track. Lexi was with him. She looked scared. Bella wished there was something she could do to help her.

Three other young ladybugs were there, too. They were wearing leg bands with numbers on them— one, two, and three.

Ladybug Three was holding a

fourth band and looking worried.

"What shall we do?" he said to the

butterfly. "The fourth member of

our team has hurt his wing and won't be able to race."

"Aha!" the butterfly said. "No need to worry. It just so happens that I have found a ladybug so fast, so fantastic, and so fabulous at flying, she will make the perfect fourth member of your team." The butterfly twirled his antennae with a flourish. "This is Lexi. She is your new Number Four!"

"Yay!" The three ladybugs

whooped and buzzed excitedly.

Bella held her breath. She wondered if they would notice that Lexi had only one spot. Lexi was obviously wondering the same thing. She was hopping from one tiny foot to the other. But the other ladybugs didn't seem to notice at all.

"You're the most important member of the team," the butterfly told Lexi. "Number Four does the last lap of the race. If you win,

you'll be the star of Sports Day."

He fixed the number four band onto Lexi's leg. Lexi fluttered her wings nervously.

"The Obstacle Relay Race is on!" the butterfly cried. "Ladybugs against June bugs. Good luck!"

"Be brave, Lexi," Bella called. "You'll be great!" She hoped Lexi could hear her.

Just then, a baby caterpillar who was sitting on his moth

mommy's back noticed Lexi
waiting behind the start line.

"Look!" he said in a loud,
surprised voice. "That ladybug's
got only one spot!"

Bella groaned. Poor Lexi!
Lexi was quite close to the little
caterpillar, so she must have heard
what he'd said. But there was
nothing Bella could do.

The yellow butterfly was giving
his instructions to the ladybug

99

team. He held up a grass seed. "Here's your baton. Pass it to the next ladybug as you finish your lap. If you don't, the team will be disqualified."

Ladybug One took the grass seed in his antennae and fluttered up to the start. He lined up next to a small green June bug.

"Ready?" the butterfly asked.

The ladybug and the June bug nodded.

"Get set!" called the butterfly.

A bumblebee flew forward.

"*ZZZZ!* GO!" she buzzed.

The two little insects flew off
so fast that their wings began to
hum. They headed for the first
obstacle—a huge pile of sticks.

Bella looked back at Lexi and
saw that her friend was sitting on
the ground, looking very frightened
indeed. With a quick hop and a
skip, Bella made her way to the

front until she was standing right next to Lexi.

"Wow, this is so exciting!" Bella said. "Three laps and then it'll be your turn."

Quivering with fear, Lexi held her front legs over her eyes. "I can't do it, Bella," she said. "Everyone will laugh at me. What am I going to do?"

CHAPTER SEVEN

Loop-the-Loop

The yellow butterfly hovered in the
air. He was holding a bright orange
mushroom shaped like a trumpet.
"They're off!" he shouted into the

mushroom. His voice echoed all over Heather Hill. "The ladybug and the June bug are coming up to the first obstacle, the sticks! And they're over!"

Bella looked down at Lexi.

Lexi was still covering her eyes.

The rest of the crowd was very excited. All the ladybugs jumped up and down. "That's our boy!" they yelled.

The June bugs jumped up and

104

down, too. "Faster!" they shouted

to the green June bug. "Go, go, go!"

Behind her, Bella could hear

the Pollen Puppies yelping with

joy. She looked back at the race.

The June bug was just entering the cobweb tunnel.

"Touch those sides, and you'll stick fast!" the butterfly cried.

Bella's whiskers twitched with excitement as the ladybug reached the tunnel.

"Number One's just about to go in," she said to Lexi, "but he's behind the June bug."

"The June bug's way out in front! He's at the last obstacle!"

106

shouted the butterfly. "There he goes, up the helter-skelter tree!"

"This bit looks really exciting," Bella said to Lexi as the June bug flew around and around between the branches of a tall tree. But Lexi still wouldn't uncover her eyes.

Bella's heart pounded as the June bug bumped into some branches. But he made it to the finish safely and back to the starting line.

"Now June Bug Two's got the baton, and he's still in the lead!" the butterfly shouted.

Ladybug One was a long way behind as he flew up to the start, holding out the grass seed for Ladybug Two.

The second ladybug was faster than the first. She raced through the tunnel so quickly, she came out ahead of the June bug!

Bella thumped her paws in glee.

Ladybug Two was brilliant!

"Look, Lexi!" Bella begged.

"She's overtaken the June bug!"

But Lexi still wouldn't look.

The butterfly roared into his

mushroom trumpet: "Ladybug Two

is coming up to the finish. Now
Ladybug Three is off!"

Bella turned to Lexi. "You're
next! Come on!"

"No, I can't!" squeaked Lexi.

Bella's ears drooped in despair.
How, oh, how could she get Lexi to
race? Then she had an idea. Bella
snuggled up close to her friend,
and she started singing a new song,
very softly, so that only Lexi could
hear.

It doesn't matter a jot

That you've got only one spot.

You can do it if you try—

All you have to do is fly!

Lexi opened her eyes and stared
at Bella. "Do you really think I can
do it?"

Bella smiled and nodded. "Of
course you can. You're wonderful at
flying."

Lexi gave a big sigh. Then,
very slowly, she stepped up to the

starting line. Everyone could see her one black spot now.

Bella knew how afraid Lexi was that everyone would laugh. But the crowd wasn't looking at Lexi. Everyone was pushing forward to see Ladybug Three as she finished her lap. She was out in front!

"Come on, ladybugs!" yelled the butterfly. "Number Three's in the lead! All she has to do is hand over to Ladybug Four. Oh no!"

There were so many creatures
milling around at the starting
line that Ladybug Three couldn't
see who to pass the baton to. She
circled in the air, searching for the
fourth member of the team.

"This way!" Bella shouted.
"Look for One-Spot Lexi!"

The sun shone down on Lexi
and her single black spot. *Now*
Ladybug Three knew who to head
for! She whizzed down toward

Lexi, holding out the grass-seed baton.

"Go, Lexi, go!" shouted Bella with a big grin.

Lexi seized the baton in her antennae and zoomed away. She was over the sticks in a flash, with a spectacular loop-the-loop.

The crowd went wild, cheering and clapping, and the Pollen Puppies wagged their tails faster than ever.

114

"We're on the last lap now. The June bugs are in the lead again. But just look at that!" howled the butterfly. "The ladybug's at the tunnel already!"

Lexi shot through the cobweb tunnel like an arrow. She was catching up to June Bug Four!

"This is amazing!" the butterfly gabbled. "Just look at One-Spot Lexi! She's loop-the-looping all the way up the helter-skelter tree!"

"Go, Lexi, *go*!" yelled Bella.

"I've never seen anything like it!" the butterfly shrieked. "She's fantabulous! She's brilltastic! She's right behind the June bug!"

Bella hopped up and down, clapping her front paws as Lexi

hurtled toward the finish. Now she

was in front of the June bug!

"Go, One-Spot Lexi! Go, go,

go!" roared the crowd.

Lexi shot across the finish line.

"Yes!" cried the butterfly,

throwing his trumpet into the air

and catching it. "She's done the fastest time ever! A Misty Wood record. The ladybugs have won!"

"I did it!" Lexi panted, circling down to land on the grass in front of Bella.

"You won! You won!" Bella was so proud of her new friend. "You're a star, Lexi!"

The rest of the ladybug team came up to congratulate Lexi.

"You were incredible!" Ladybug

One said. "We'd never have won without you."

The yellow butterfly called the team over to collect their prizes. He gave each ladybug an acorn cup full of golden honey.

"Well done, One-Spot Lexi," he said.

Lexi blushed even redder. She took her honey and hurried back to Bella.

"Let's get away before they

start laughing at my spot,"
she said, looking around at the
spectators who were still buzzing
with excitement about the race.

The two friends fluttered their
wings and drifted away over the
heather, looking for somewhere
quiet. But everywhere they went,
insects and fairy animals flew up to
congratulate Lexi.

"Hello!" called a Moss Mouse.
"I loved your loop-the-loops!" He

tried a clumsy loop of his own
before flying off.

"Mmmarvelous!" droned
a furry bee. "Bbbbessst race
evvvvverr!" Then she buzzed away,
searching for a flower.

"They're not laughing at me!"
Lexi said, looking very surprised.

"Why would they laugh?" Bella
said with a smile. She saw a patch
of grass between the heather plants.
"Let's go and sit over there so you

can eat some of your prize honey."

"You have to have some, too," Lexi said. "If it wasn't for you, I'd never have been brave enough to race."

They flew down and were just dipping into the acorn when a very small ladybug peeped at them through the heather stalks.

He looked at Lexi shyly. "Hello, Lexi. You're my hero," he mumbled, then darted away.

Lexi stared after him. Then she looked at Bella, puzzled. "Why would he say that I'm his hero?"

"Because you won the race for the ladybug team," Bella said. "And it wasn't *just* because you're so good at flying."

"What do you mean?" Lexi asked.

Bella licked a drop of delicious honey from her paw. "Well, if you weren't One-Spot Lexi, Ladybug

Three would never have known who to pass the baton to."

Lexi looked thoughtful. Then her eyes began to shine. "You mean . . . it was a *good* thing that I have only one spot?"

Bella nodded. A smile spread slowly across Lexi's face, and she zoomed up into the air in a happy loop-the-loop. "Maybe being different isn't so bad after all," she called down to Bella. "Wheeeeeee!"

There was a shimmer of silver wings above the heather, and Carla the Cobweb Kitten fluttered down to join them.

"Hello, Bella! I've been looking for you everywhere," she said. "Did you see the Obstacle Relay Race? It was amazing!"

"Yes," Bella said proudly. She nodded at Lexi. "My new friend here just won it."

"Oh, wow!" Carla looked at

125

Lexi with admiration. "You were brilliant. I wish I could do loop-the-loops like you."

"I can teach you if you like," Lexi said shyly.

"Ooh, really?" Carla fluttered her silver wings excitedly. "I would love that!"

Carla turned back to Bella. "Are you still trying to find out where spots come from?"

Bella looked at Lexi.

Lexi smiled and shook her head. She was happy just the way she was.

"Not anymore," Bella said, winking at Lexi. "No need for more spots here!"

127

The sun was starting to hide his face behind the trees of Misty Wood, and the sky was turning golden pink. The warm spring day was coming to an end. It was nearly time to go home.

"Thank you, Bella," said Lexi. "Your songs have really helped me today."

"You're welcome," Bella said. "In fact . . ."

Bella began hopping around

128

Lexi and Carla as she started

singing another song.

Making friends with you

Has been the best thing by far.

One-Spot Lexi,

The loop-the-loop star!

Misty Wood Word Search

Can you find all these words from
the story in this fun word search?

BELLA   HOP   RACE
BUNNY   LEXI   SKIP
FlOWER   PETAL WINGS

```
X T O N F B U N N Y L V T
R P E R B R A C E E A L C
C J R B H V F A W T X H K
H N V S D G L H L I H O P
W A D G F L O W E R N I M
D Z E C E R L I T K G Q
Y D X B M X W G K S L F S
B N U V E I E W P H A N K
P E T A L E K L U L L P
```

Help Bella finish her song!

Bella loves singing about Misty Wood! She was making up a new song when she had to hop off to Bluebell Glade to open some buds.

Help Bella finish her song in the lines below.

I love skipping over the hill.
To skip, skip, skip
Gives me a thrill!

I love hopping in the sun.
To hop, hop, hop
Is so much fun!

_____

_____

_____

Help Lexi find her way
to the finish line.

Watch out for dead ends!

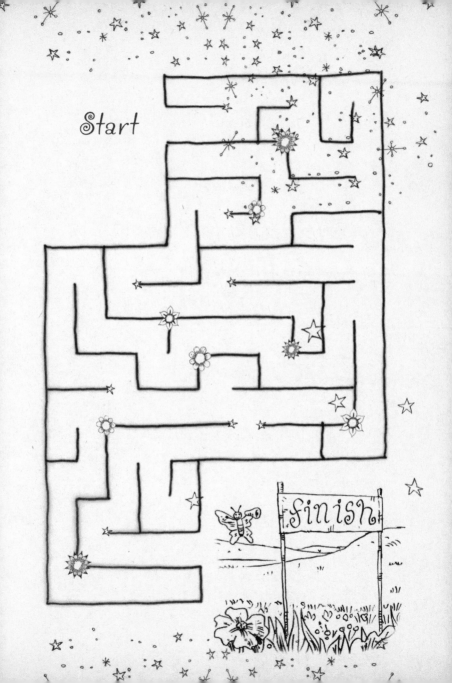

Fairy Animals
of Misty Wood

Meet more Fairy Animal friends!